ALPHA'S OMEGA

JUNO WELLS

of the author's imagination. Please note that this work is intended only for adults over the age of 18 and all characters represented as 18 or over.

Cover by Amourisa Designs

BLURB

Omega Maya keeps to herself working the fringes of known space to salvage derelict ships and other resources. She wants nothing to do with Alphas, so when Remy shows up at her current salvage operation, she's at first displeased. He soon starts to win her over, but when her suppressant stops working, and he realizes she's an Omega, he's intent on claiming her. Maya doesn't want to be any Alpha's Omega, even Remy's. Can she enjoy the pleasure he offers without surrendering everything she is and believes in or succumbing to her biological imperative to submit?

Remy's been searching for his Omega for years, and he's convinced he's found her in Maya. She stirs his need to love and protect, and it pains him that she doesn't want what he's offering. He understands the traumas in her past, but can he help her overcome them to embrace a future together?

CHAPTER ONE

"Son of a…" muttered Maya Broward to herself as she struggled to disengage the chunk of scrap metal she was cutting from the hull of the derelict ship. It was being particularly stubborn, but she wanted the panel if she could get it to come off since it contained several rare metals that comprised the alloys used to make this model of freighter.

"Did you say something?" asked Swish.

Maya glanced away from the

cutting, not bothering to remove the shielding option of her visor on the E-suit, since she would be back to looking at the laser cutting again in a moment. "Nothing, Swish. I was just talking to myself."

The CAP—computerized autonomous pet—jumped higher onto a spot on the hull. Since Swish was a mechanized organism, "she" required no protection against the space around them. "It's a sign of insanity to talk to yourself."

In spite of her irritation with the job ahead of her, Maya laughed. "It's only insane if you also answer. Besides, I talk to you.

Does that make me crazy?"

Swish tilted her head, staring at Maya with her catlike eyes set in the feline-shaped configuration Maya had chosen when she purchased the CAP solar cycles ago. "There's an argument to be made that you are, and you aren't. It's perfectly normal for people to talk to pets, but I suppose one could consider me an inanimate object."

Maya laughed and shook her head again as she returned her attention to cutting the hull. "If you're inanimate, so am I. You talk more than I do."

"I'm simply responding to the program settings you chose."

With a sniff and a stretch that was entirely catlike, Swish climbed a little higher on the hull, clinging easily with the magnetic option built into her paws. She observed in silent judgment as Maya continued to struggle with the piece of metal, finally getting it to cut loose and peel away once she hit it with a ultrasonic charge that briefly disrupted its molecules.

It was a heavy piece of hull, but since they were in space, with no atmosphere, it was easy enough to move from the hull to her skid nearby using the thrusters in her E-suit. Maya put it on the skid, glad to see her pile was growing.

The CAP's eyes flashed red for a

second. "Computer is indicating there's a ship approaching," said Swish, looking completely alert and no longer languid. She knew how Maya felt about visitors or any type of social interaction.

Maya froze, her first instinct to panic and run for her ship, *Eve's Sacrifice*. If she took the skid, they could be back in less than five minutes. If she abandoned it, she could be at her ship in two minutes and ready to take off within five minutes more.

It took every bit of strength she had to quell the instinct to run. If she took off without so much as a piece of the scrap metal she had spent most the morning salvaging, she'd be leaving with a virtually empty hold. That wouldn't even cover the cost of fuel to travel to the Antares Belt, not to mention losing out on all the wreckage around them. Far too many people had recklessly considered themselves capable enough pilots to tackle the Antares Asteroid Belt, and a great number of them had found out to their detriment they were wrong.

These days, travel through the belt was restricted, but there was a veritable ships' graveyard around from the previous travelers. It was a source of income she desperately needed.

Maya used her thrusters to

climb on top of the pile of scrap metal in case she decided she needed to beat a hasty retreat after all. "Swish, have the computer signal the newcomer."

"Yes, Maya." The CAP was silent for a moment, clearly communing with the computer on *Eve's Sacrifice*. She nodded at Maya a moment later. Maya took a deep breath and brought up her wrist comm so she could view whoever awaited her.

She caught her breath when a handsome face filled her screen. She couldn't be certain without seeing all of his body, but judging from the broadness of his shoulders and the sheer perfection of his features, coupled with the long black hair and warm brown eyes that provided the only touch of softness in his face, she suspected he was an Alpha.

A shudder went through her, and her hand automatically dropped to the discreet pump on her hip, reminding herself it was there and fully functioning. He wouldn't know what she was.

He smiled at her, and it was a devastating grin. It caused her heart to race, and Maya felt the first stirrings of arousal in years. Rather than please her, that left her mouth dry and her palms sweating. Fortunately, the E-suit wicked away the moisture for recycling, and she was able to maintain what she hoped was a calm exterior when she started speaking. "I've already placed a claim on this sector."

"As did I when I arrived. I'm sure you're aware that per Coalition regulations, you can only claim salvage ships which you are actively engaged in salvaging."

She glared at him. "I was here first."

His eyes widened, and he seemed surprised at her response. "Surely, there are plenty for both of us."

She looked around, biting her lip for a moment. Technically, he was right. They were surrounded by dozens of wrecks, and since the Antares Belt was so far away from the central Coalition planets, just at the edge of known space, not many salvagers made it this way. With a sigh of defeat, she nodded her head just once. "Very well. Just stay out of my way."

He seemed surprised again, and she imagined he wasn't used to women being so abrupt with him. No doubt, he had every Beta female throwing herself at his feet, and probably even a few Alphas. If he could find an Omega, she would be his slavering slave—unless she were Maya, who had no intention of being any Alpha's

Omega.

"I'm sorry if I've offended you. If we work together, we could probably accomplish the task much faster and split the proceeds?"

She maintained her stony expression. "As I said, just stay out of my way." Without another word, she pressed the button to disconnect the communication, and his face disappeared from her wrist comm. Once he could no longer see her, she let out a heavy sigh and trembled a little. Then she let out a startled screech when Swish rubbed against her leg in a soothing fashion. She hadn't realized she'd made the trip from the salvage ship to the skid. "Warn a lady."

Swish looked up at her with concern. "You're all right, Maya?" The CAP had no snark in her tone. She was clearly worried about her mistress.

With a sigh, Maya nodded and bent down, scratching the CAP behind the ear. Swish was programmed to respond to reward behavior and stimuli just like a normal pet would, and her purr vibrated Maya's hand through the E-suit.

Still feeling somewhat shaken by the encounter, Maya forced herself to return to the ship. She put Swish on guard duty, ensuring she would warn her if the man with whom she shared the space tried to approach. So far, he had remained a respectable distance away, engaging artificial orbit, but keeping space between his ship, the *Raven*, and *Eve's Sacrifice*. She liked it that way, and it allowed her to relax enough to finish working.

Three hours later, she'd stripped all she could for now as she neared the point of exhaustion, and Maya decided to call it a day. She had enough to partially fill the cargo hold now, and with what she'd recovered, if she got a fair price, she could pay her expenses for another few months.

It wasn't all that she'd hoped to acquire while she was here, since it'd taken her a while to save enough money for the fuel and ionospace boost gate fees and was supposed to be a big haul, but if she had to make a hasty retreat, at least she wasn't leaving empty-handed now.

After guiding the skid back to her ship and using the automated system aboard to unload it, she parked it for the evening and ensured the hold was locked tight with her biometric print before walking through the ship. *Eve's Sacrifice* was small by most standards, but that allowed her to easily pilot it with the help of the state-of-the-art A.I. autopilot system. She'd put quite a lot into ensuring the ship could function with just her, since she wanted no companion or copilot. Swish was as close as she got to sharing her space, and that was plenty for her.

She went to her quarters and stripped off, intent on a shower before eating. The E-suit did a good job of wicking away perspiration and keeping her cool, but she still felt grimy, so it was a relief to step into the cool shower, and she shivered as the water chilled her before slowly warming to her preferred temperature. It was a defect in the shower that she had to fix someday, but it was a low priority.

As she washed, Maya couldn't help thinking about the Alpha sharing her space. She couldn't be certain he was until she saw him and confirmed he had the hard muscles and larger build of the typical Alpha, but from what she'd seen, she wouldn't be surprised to discover he was. It was bad enough somebody had disturbed her solitude, but to discover she had to share space with an Alpha left her feeling slightly nauseated.

Her nausea only increased when she recalled her physical response at the sight of him. It wasn't like Maya to feel attraction for anyone, but particularly Alphas. After her experience in the past, she couldn't imagine a situation where she would ever willingly submit to an Alpha, so she steered clear of them. That, combined with her suppressant, let her lead a relatively normal, if mostly asexual, life that contented her.

So why had she responded to him? It was upsetting, and as soon as she was out of the shower, Maya wrapped a towel around herself and went into the bedroom attached to the bathroom, opening a drawer to take out a handheld scanner. She used it to check the state of her pump, finding it was functioning at nominal levels. The dosage of suppressant hadn't lessened, so there was no good explanation for why she was drawn to the Alpha, however reluctantly. She reinforced her resolve to steer clear of him as much as possible.

CHAPTER TWO

Remy Cruz had already picked the freighter he planned to start salvage on the next morning, and he was on the way to it with his skid when he saw the woman from yesterday approaching on her skid as well. He considered it a happy accident, though he suspected she would accuse him of infringing on her find. The problem was, he'd already registered his claim for this vessel before departing the ship.

Their skids reached the wreckage of the ship *Januvia* at

roughly the same moment. Her hands were already on her hips, and as she approached him riding her skid, he couldn't help thinking she was beautiful. She stirred his interest, though it was impossible to tell if she was an Omega with their E-suits blocking their scents.

Unlike with Alphas, an Omega's stature wasn't necessarily any shorter or smaller than Betas, so he couldn't tell just by visual appraisal. The way she made his pulse rocket had him considering the possibility that she might be though. He didn't usually take notice of Betas much these days, focused as he was on finding his true Omega.

She was certainly beautiful, with pale skin that suggested she hadn't spent enough time in her UV chamber, closely cropped chestnut-colored curls, and unusual purple-blue eyes that were vivid even from the distance separating them and with both wearing helmets.

She had a CAP with her, and it jumped from the woman's skid to his even as she waved it back. He looked down at the feline-bot and nodded his head. "Hello."

The CAP stared at him appraisingly for a long second. "Change your communication frequency to channel eight-seven-two." With those instructions, it seamlessly jumped from his skid back to the woman's.

He did as instructed, and soon enough, the woman's voice was filling his head. It was just as pleasing and dulcet as yesterday, except for the tone of outrage that lent a shrill pitch. "How dare you? This is my find."

"I identified it earlier this morning via scan. It has some of the richest deposits of rathium. I've already registered a claim." Inasmuch as he wanted to please her, as he would want to any woman, since it was in his nature to care for those who weren't Alphas, he wasn't going to give up on the find.

She scowled at him. "I've already claimed it as well. It was part of the scan I did last week when determining my working order."

He arched a brow. "There must've been a problem with your claim then, or the system would have refused mine."

She looked disconcerted, and her voice lowered a bit, as though she were mumbling. "I just registered it this morning."

He nodded, not surprised, since she would have been bending the laws if she'd registered it that much in advance of working on it. "What time?"

She shrugged a shoulder. "Maybe thirteen minutes ago? It was shortly before I left the ship."

He couldn't help a grin. "I suspect we might've registered at the same time. Why don't you check your status while I check mine?" She gave him a grudging nod and lowered her head as he brought up his wrist comm.

He called up his claim history and was unsurprised to see he was listed as the co-owner of the salvage now, sharing the find with one Maya Broward. Now he had a name for her. He looked up, giving her a slow grin. "It appears we registered our claim at the same time."

Her shoulders slumped, and she nodded. "Very well. I'll withdraw mine."

"No," he said forcefully, making her flinch. He immediately lowered his voice, taking on a gentler tone. "There's no need for that. There are plenty of items to share. I suggest we work together to recover it. This is just an accident, but we might as will make the best of it."

She bit her lip, looking indecisive for a moment. The CAP brushed against her leg, and it seemed to be in a reassuring fashion that worked, because Maya squared her shoulders and nodded. "Very well, Mr. Cruz. I'll take the aft end if you want to take the forward end."

That wasn't what he'd envisioned. He'd had plans of working alongside her, but if this were all she was willing to do, he considered it a minor victory. With a nod of his head, he directed the skid toward his half of the ship while she moved around to the other side.

That meant he lost sight of her, but he could still talk to her, and he spent the next several minutes doing so as he started to work. He quickly discovered either she wasn't much of a conversationalist, or she just didn't want to talk to him, but he didn't let that deter him. Remy had always been loquacious, and it was kind of fun to have a captive audience, especially when he knew she was fighting not to respond. He could tell by the way she drew in her breath sometimes, and by the note of irritation in her voice when she did answer.

"How long have you been here?"

"A couple of weeks," she said after a hesitation.

"It takes a while to get here, huh?"

"It's a long trip. And it took a while to save for the fuel expenses and the tolls to use the ionospace booster gate."

He nodded. "I know what you mean. I've been flying solo for about a year now, and I just finally got enough together to make this trek. I need to make it a successful one."

She sighed, and he couldn't tell if she was irritated with him, or if she was empathetic. Her tone had softened slightly when she said, "So do I."

"It's a good thing there's plenty to work with around here. I still think we might want to consider teaming up. We could get it done faster."

Her silence spoke volumes.

He uttered a small sigh of his own. "Is it just you and the CAP?"

"Swish," said the CAP.

"That's how I like it," she said with a hint of defensiveness just after the pet's reply.

He paused, forced to take a break from conversation as the laser cutter seemed like it might overheat. It took a moment to restore its cooling function, and then he could focus on her again. "It's different traveling alone. Before this, I was part of a crew of what I thought were traders, but they turned out to be more."

She sounded reluctantly intrigued. "How so?"

"I discovered their second hold on the ship by accident. It was filled with weapons and contraband, and I don't fancy spending the rest of my life in a Coalition hellhole prison, so I left the crew as soon as we stopped at the next port."

He grimaced, calling how overbearing Aurelius Stahl had been. As captain of the *Aurelius*, named for the captain himself and a true reflection of the other Alpha's arrogance, he'd expected final word on everything. Remy was already chafing at accepting Aurelius's authority, and he'd been considering the idea of leaving the crew, but finding the illegal cargo hold filled with weapons that didn't belong in anyone's hands had hastened his decision, though he imagined it had angered Aurelius. Not because he lost a viable crewmember, but simply because Remy had gone his own way without consulting the other Alpha. That wasn't Remy's style. He did what he wanted, and he tended to live and let live whenever possible.

"It sounds like you made a good decision."

He liked her validation, though he certainly didn't need it. "I think so. I worked some odd jobs on that planet for a while until I had enough to buy the freighter. Then I took some smaller salvage jobs until I had enough accumulated to make the trip to the Antares Belt."

"I guess our stories are similar." She sounded pained to reveal anything about herself.

He wanted to ask more, like how she'd ended up alone out here, and if it was by choice, but he sensed she wouldn't respond well to any personal questions. Instead, he said, "One's gotta make a living, huh?"

"Indeed. The idea of living in one of the Coalition cities on the major planets holds no appeal to me."

"Me neither. I'm glad to be away from all that." He shuddered at the thought. They were overcrowded, and while they were technically clean, there was just underneath the surface an air of grime about most of them that made his skin crawl. He preferred the vast expanse of empty space to the overcrowded cities on most Coalition planets.

Out here, he could do what he wanted when he wanted. For him, that kept things simple. It wasn't to hurt anyone or break any laws. He just wanted to be left alone to find his Omega and make a living doing what he chose rather than being assigned some Coalition task or put on the Coalition dole.

There was more warmth in her tone when she said, "I'm not surprised. Most people who grow up in those places all their lives never find their way out though." Her voice rang with pride.

He was intrigued, but he forced himself not to ask any questions. "I've lived on a few of the planets here and there but never could get comfortable and feel at home."

"I mostly grew up in the New Bacar colony." Her voice was clipped. "I wouldn't recommend it."

"I've actually been there. If I recall, it's one of the more overpopulated, less hygienic places." She laughed, and the sound was musical, causing his insides to contort in a strange fashion that left him feeling breathless.

"I suppose it's not overly dirty, but it feels like it is with all the people crammed in together, along with the dissatisfaction and unhappiness. So many people there are on the dole due to lack of economic opportunities and poor resources that it leads to frustration and violence. The enforcers were quick to crack down, but they couldn't keep it from happening."

He heard a little fear in her voice then, and he was convinced she spoke from familiarity. Remy wanted to ask more, but since she was talking to him, he didn't want to risk her closing down.

Instead, he changed the subject to tell her about some of the other places he'd lived throughout his life, starting with the cities before moving on to some of his other adventures. As long as they kept things relatively impersonal, she was a willing conversationalist, and they passed the day working together companionably.

Near lunchtime, he asked, "Are you going back to your ship for food?"

"No. I have a nutrition pack in my suit."

He frowned at the dart of disappointment, though he had done the same. When planning to ingest lunch via his suit, he hadn't considered the possibility he might be able to sit down and share a meal with someone instead. "Yeah, me too. I plan to just work through lunch."

"Same."

Those were the last words exchanged for another hour or so as she got busy disassembling a particularly stubborn part of the ship and was unable to focus long enough to talk. He respected that, not wanting her to injure herself by him distracting her, so he waited until he saw her appear around the side with her skid before he started speaking again.

It was mostly idle chitchat, but he could catch glimpses of the real her revealed by her tone. He was dying to have her take off her E-suit so he could smell her. He wanted to find an Omega, the perfect one for him, and if she wasn't an Omega, he was going to be sorely disappointed.

Remy had decided a couple of years ago that he no longer wanted to pursue casual sex with Betas or other Alphas when his Omega was out there waiting. They were rare, but he intended to find her, so he had devoted himself to that task while making a living. For the first time in the two years since deciding his next lover would only be his Omega, he was tempted to break from the idea if this woman was a Beta.

When they had finished for the day, she came with her skid to stand near him again, though a few feet of space separated them. She was closer than she had been this morning, and she appeared far more relaxed. That decided him to say, "You could come over to my ship for a meal, if you want?"

Her expression closed, and she crossed her arms over her chest. "Thanks, but I have plans."

He arched a brow, knowing it was a lie, and at least she had the grace to blush. He could tell that from the heat sensors in his suit that lit up around her face.

"Going to the symphony?"

She laughed, though it was a little awkward. "I meant I already have a meal prepared and waiting for me. Thank you for the invitation"

It was clearly a refusal, and he decided to accept graciously and not seem like a pushy Alpha. "I thought we worked well together today. Did you?"

She nodded after a short hesitation. "It wasn't bad at all. For some reason, I feel like I accomplished more, though I would've done the same amount of work either way."

He nodded his agreement. "I think it's because having someone to talk to helps pass the time. What do you think about working together tomorrow? I was going to go after the…" He trailed off for a minute to bring up the analysis report he had done upon his arrival yesterday. "*Helena* tomorrow."

She looked at her wrist comm and hesitated for a moment before nodding. "I had another ship on the list first, but that's agreeable. I was saving the *Helena* for later, since it's such a large project."

"I think we can make short work of it between the two of us. We'll have to go inside the ship though. Its ionocore is still functional according to my analysis."

She nodded. "I see that as well. Do you have the expertise to disassemble it? I've never done that before."

"I do. I spent some time working in a repair hub on a planet."

"That should definitely be your claim then."

He frowned, realizing what a substantial amount it was. That was part of what had drawn him to it. Only the rathium they had harvested today was worth more in this graveyard of ships. "I wouldn't feel right doing that."

She shrugged a shoulder. "I had no plans to salvage it myself, since

I don't know how, so you aren't taking it from me. I'll be happy to help if you need it, and in return, I'll take a little more of the other salvage. Deal?"

He still felt like he was giving her an unfair bargain, but it was her suggestion, so he shrugged. "If you're happy with that, then yes."

She nodded at him. "In that case, I'll see you in the morning. I like to get started early."

"So do I." He lifted his hand and waved at her as her skid headed back to her ship. She didn't glance back, to his regret. He could look into her purplish eyes for hours, and he reluctantly put his skid in gear and directed it toward his ship, separating from her once more. He'd hoped the evening would end differently.

Once he arrived on the *Raven* and had secured his cargo for the day and stowed his skid, he moved through the ship to his quarters, ravenous but also wanting to clean up. He stepped into a hot shower moments later, closing his eyes as the water beat down over him. It felt wonderfully refreshing, helping to ease some of the soreness in his muscles from the day's hard work, and he slumped against the wall.

It wasn't a conscious choice. Her face just appeared before him, without the E-suit. In his fantasy, she was an Omega, and she smelled delicious. In real life, Remy groaned as he cupped his cock in his hand, starting to stroke himself as he imagined what it would be like to bury his face against one of the scent glands in her neck and inhale, before rubbing against her to impart his scent.

He imagined her skin flushed with estrus, filled with a frantic need to have him as she tugged at his clothes that magically disappeared in the fantasy, leaving him as naked then as he was in real life. She was naked too, and her reddish nipples were particularly luscious, her estrus making them seem like delicious cherries. He moaned as he imagined the taste of them in his mouth while stroking his cock harder.

In the fantasy, his mouth drifted from her nipple down her body, finding her wet core. She was drenched with slick that would ease the way for his Alpha cock. First, he had to ensure she was ready for him, so he would dip his tongue inside, tasting her until she came in his mouth, filling him with her slick before he lifted her, lined up his cock, and drove into the heat of her.

He squeezed his fist around his cock as he imagined what it would be like to be inside his Omega. Generally, his fantasy Omegas had a more generic appearance, since he hadn't met an Omega in years, and the last ones had been claimed by others. That automatically made them unappealing, even for fantasies.

This time, he could clearly see Maya's face and imagined it was her pussy he was driving into. He didn't knot as he came, since he wasn't inside his Omega during her estrus, so the orgasm was only partially satisfying, and it didn't last nearly as long as it would if he had been engaged with his mate.

It took the edge off though, allowing him to finish his shower and step out a short time later. He tried not to think about Maya or the fantasy he had created in his mind. He prayed she would be an Omega, but until he had a chance to get the E-suit off her, he wouldn't know.

He was going to be vastly disappointed if she was just another Beta. He was so drawn to her, but he wasn't certain he could be happy with a Beta when he could have an Omega. There was just something missing in such a relationship, and he wasn't willing to compromise even for someone as alluring as Maya.

CHAPTER THREE

Her heart had dropped when she first saw him yesterday and confirmed he was an Alpha. She'd wanted to run away, but she'd managed to stay and stake her claim. Maya was still nervous about working with him today, but he was clearly competent, and the day had gone faster. He'd respected her boundaries, and with the suppressant doing its job, he'd never know she was an Omega. As long as she didn't seem like anything special to him, he was likely to leave her alone.

It didn't keep her from arming herself with a laser pistol and a taser, just to be on the safe side. They would be working together inside the ship and in closer quarters today, and she intended to make sure she could protect herself if the need arose.

She knew how it would go for her if she ended up shooting an Alpha, since it had happened to her brother, but she wasn't going to be passive and not defend herself as the need arose. She was still trembling slightly when she drank her morning coffee, and Swish jumped onto the table with her, rubbing against her arm in a soothing fashion.

She had no doubt Swish had all the knowledge of her past history, since the CAP interfaced with the computer and had access to records. They were programmed to do so, in order to become better companions, so she assumed Swish knew everything and understood why she was nervous. "Am I doing the right thing?"

"You're doing the sensible thing. You work well with him, and I believe you were more productive than usual."

Maya nodded at the CAP's assessment. "Yeah, I was." She'd had to concede that when she got back to her cargo hold yesterday and realized she had recovered ten percent more than she had guesstimated based on her previous efforts. "He's an Alpha."

"He seems like a nice one."

Maya gripped her coffee cup hard for a moment before managing to relax her grip and take a deep breath. "Yeah, he does, if there's such thing as a *nice* Alpha. He doesn't know what I am though."

"Maybe he won't care if he finds out." Swish turned her head in a curious fashion. "Is that a possibility? You've interacted with Alphas before."

"Thanks to the suppressant." Feeling paranoid, Maya took a

moment to run another diagnostic on it to ensure it was working properly before returning her dishes to the washer so the ship could clean and put them away. After that, there was nothing left to do except don her E-suit, hop on the skid, and fly it out to meet Remy where he was waiting for her at the *Helena*.

When she arrived, she managed a smile, which wasn't hard to do, since he was beaming at her. He seemed pleased to see her, and she couldn't deny she was happy to see him as well. Maybe she was a little lonelier than she would admit to herself out here in space with just Swish for company. She had to be if she was considering an Alpha a viable working companion.

"How did you sleep?" he asked.

She shrugged. "Fine." She moved the skid closer to the breach in the hull. "And you?"

"Very well." There was a hint of smokiness in his tone, and for a moment, his eyes gleamed with pure male appreciation.

It made her nervous, and she quickly looked away. "It seems like there might be some atmosphere aboard."

"That's what my sensors tell me. I suggest we go to Maintenance first to see if we can get atmosphere online, along with gravity. If we get those to work, it will make salvaging easier."

Maya was agreeable, and it would've been her first stop even if she was salvaging alone. She couldn't always repair such things, but sometimes she'd managed in the past. It was always easier to do her job when she didn't have to wear the E-suit and could rely on light from the ship rather than light she brought herself.

They parked their skids side-by-side, and he held out a hand to assist her inside the hole in the side of the hull. Maya gasped softly when she took his hand, doing her best to hide any reaction. She shouldn't feel any flair of heat with both of them in E-suits, which made pheromones impossible to detect, but her heartrate definitely increased. She touched her hip almost subconsciously, patting the pump there.

He followed behind her, and Swish jumped in last. Maya allowed Remy to take the lead, understanding he would naturally want to as an Alpha. His nature would be to protect, which sounded good, but she didn't want to be smothered by a possessive Alpha. Nor did she want to be used like a toy to be discarded or taken advantage of during estrus, which lowered her inhibitions. It was far safer to live on the suppressant as her mother had done.

They had to clear some debris to get through the corridor but soon found the maintenance deck, and working together, had the internal atmosphere running a short time later. Lights came on, and a heavy sensation dragged down on her as the ship restored gravity. Maya used her wrist comm to disengage the gravity from her E-suit, so she felt normal again.

"We don't have much oxygen in this room, but it appears once we get past thise section and seal the area, we can remove our E-suits."

"Or at least the helmet." Maya smiled at him she said that, glad to be rid of the thing. It was confining, and though it had excellent airflow, she sometimes still felt like she was on the verge of a panic attack when she'd worn it for too long.

They proceeded down a corridor that was also strewn with debris from the wreck, identifying several points of asteroid entry. The ship must've been battered by several asteroids from the belt, though the latter half of it appeared to be mostly intact. Unfortunately for the people aboard, the asteroids had damaged critical systems that left it a drifting derelict.

A few minutes later, her wrist comm beeped to indicate they had atmosphere, and she nodded to Remy as he closed the section behind them, sealing off that part of the hull and leaving them in a self-contained space. After another moment to allow for oxygen to reach full capacity, she reached up to undo the thin helmet, pulling it back and taking in a deep breath.

The room smelled musty, but she wasn't surprised. It had been floating for at least thirty years, and it was a miracle some of the systems still worked.

When she breathed deeply, she caught another scent over the old mustiness. It was the delicious aroma of an Alpha, and she shuddered as his pheromones hit her. It took everything she had to remain upright and not moan. Instead, she slumped partially against the wall to support herself for a moment as his enticing aroma wafted over her.

The suppressant filtered out most of its impact, thankfully dulling her senses, but it was still enough to make her weak in the knees. She was unaccustomed to reacting that way to any Alpha, and she sent him a look filled with curiosity and a little fear. What was so different about this Alpha?

He was eyeing her and sniffing,

at first with a gleam in his eyes that slowly faded. His shoulders slumped forward a moment later, and he appeared disappointed. It was only a guess, but Maya assumed his reaction was because he didn't detect her as an Omega, and she had to bite hard on her tongue to resist revealing her secret. It was safer for everyone if she maintained the charade of being a Beta. No matter how good he smelled, he was still an Alpha. She knew how they could be, and she wanted no part of that.

Clearing her throat, she said, "Shall we get on with it then?"

He nodded his agreement, once again leading the way with the schematics from his wrists comm.

Maya followed behind him, ensuring his coordinates and path matched the one her ship's A.I. had mapped out as well, soon satisfied he was going the right way. That led them through a series of twists and turns before they reached the ionocore. Once again, they both put on their helmets before entering, just as a precaution against any contaminants that might be leaking. The ship had been sitting for thirty years, so it was better to be prudent.

She was impressed with how quickly he disassembled the core. He didn't bother trying to take the whole thing, of course. He was only after the ionocore that powered the ship's system. She assisted him a little, but mostly she spent her time salvaging other parts of the room and adding them to the bag she'd removed from her back.

She admired from a distance as his muscles bulged even through the E-suit, which fit him like a glove. He was certainly an impressive specimen, and more than once, her gaze dropped to his cock, though she was ashamed of herself for the curiosity.

She knew having an Alpha take her would be nothing but pain, so she couldn't understand her uncharacteristic curiosity about his length or speculation about how it would feel to have him inside her. She must be approaching estrus, but that made no sense either. The pump would automatically adjust the dose to counter the increase in hormones and pheromones that accompanied it. No, there was something about the man himself and had nothing to do with her pump malfunctioning.

For the briefest moment, she entertained the idea that he might be her true Alpha, one that was an ideal match for her. It was mostly a fairytale that she believed Alphas told themselves as they searched for their Omegas, and it allowed Omegas to believe they were more than a commodity for the right Alpha. She held no stock in it, and she shook her head to dismiss the naïve theory almost as soon as it came to her mind.

A few minutes later, he asked, "Will you help me lift this?"

With a nod, she moved over, grasping one side of the core as he took the other. It was relatively small, but dense and heavy. With a grunt, she lifted her part, and he lifted the lion's share. Together, they managed to get it in the bag he'd brought. He sealed it inside, and she was pleased to see he'd brought a shielded sack to protect them from possible contaminant leakage. He seemed to know exactly what he was doing.

Would that expertise carry through to the bedroom? She shook her head at the thought, disgusted with herself and frowning.

He looked up then, his expression confused. "Is something wrong?"

She cleared her throat. "I…uh… No. Why?"

He shrugged a shoulder. "You seemed upset for a moment. Are you certain you don't want to claim half the value of the ionocore? I'm sure we can find a way to split the proceeds."

Maya made herself smile. "No, I don't care about it. You did most of the work, and I'm happy with what I've managed to scrounge from this room. However, there is a terilalium source that I'd like to go after a few decks up."

He looked surprised. "Terilalium? My analysis shows none."

She shrugged. "Perhaps I have better A.I." She could guarantee it, considering the cost of her program, which she kept up to date at all times.

"It sounds like it, but why would terilalium be on the ship?"

She shrugged. "It's located in an area designated as quarters, so I assume it belonged to a rich passenger aboard. It's likely some necklace or bauble, and it should provide fuel for at least half a solar cycle."

He grinned. "In that case, I don't feel so bad about taking the ionocore."

She frowned. "I plan to cut it in half and share it."

He waved a hand. "No, whatever terilalium we find is yours."

She was pleased by that, finding him thoughtful and protective. He was everything an Alpha should be, or he appeared to be, but she knew how deceptive they could be. She couldn't afford to lower her guard or trust any of them, even when he seemed like the decent sort, such as Remy.

They moved through the ship, soon diverting to a conduit. "We don't have any choice but to climb. The main route is blocked with debris and a sealed hull door to keep the hull breach from affecting the area." He delivered the report as he read his wrist comm.

Her E-suit gave similar results, and she nodded. "I'll go first."

He growled low in his throat. "I'll go first."

She rolled her eyes as she fastened her helmet again for added protection. "I have a smaller build than you, and I can wiggle through debris if needed easier than you can." Without waiting for his agreement, she grasped the rungs of the ladder and started climbing the conduit. She heard him mutter low in his throat and issue a very Alpha-like growl as she passed by him, climbing upward, but he didn't argue. He was soon following behind her, close enough to be a reassuring presence, but not so close that she was afraid she would step on his hand or inadvertently brush against him in the dark.

The area wasn't completely dark, but the dim lighting provided by the ship's auxiliary power for the section was hardly what she called illuminating. It provided enough light to ensure that everyone on the ladder was there, and it also revealed a section of debris above. She groaned as she reached for her cutting tool, analyzing the positioning for a moment and discerning she could cut a path through for them if she got the right angle.

"What are you doing?" asked Remy through the headset built into his E-suit.

"Just removing some of this debris." She blocked him out for a moment as she focused on obtaining the proper angle, starting to cut through the metal above her. The tool sliced through relatively easily, but she must've miscalculated, because as the two pieces started the split, one of them shifted and fell downward, rushing right for her.

She recoiled, pulling herself into a ball and covering her head as the metal crashed around her, hitting her in the side and sending her sliding down several rungs. She would've fallen hard if Remy hadn't reached out and grasped her arm, pulling her against him.

For a moment, she forgot all about anything else except the feel of the Alpha's arms around her. She stared up at him uncertainly, licking her lips. He groaned in response, and if it hadn't been for the debris crashing to the ground beneath them distracting them, they might've stayed like that indefinitely.

Clearing her throat, she reached out to grasp a rung with her other hand. "Thank you."

He nodded. "No problem. Do we need to turn back?"

She looked at her wrist comm as she climbed again. "No, I think we can squeeze through." A second later, she emerged onto the next deck, kicking aside the debris she had cut so he could have enough room to push through too. She quickly moved on to the next ladder, taking that conduit all the way to the area from where the terilalium pinged on her scanner. Once safely out of the conduit, she unfastened her helmet.

The quarters were lit with auxiliary power too, so the lighting was dimmer, which made it a little harder to find their way. She nearly tripped on something, but his hand on her shoulder from behind kept her steady.

At that point, he moved around in front of her, shielding her from harm from the front. They reached the pertinent quarters a moment later, and he made short work of opening the door with a prybar and a sonic disruptor that loosened the bond of the molecules in the metal. The door slid open with a tortured groan, and he stepped inside.

Maya followed behind him, nearly overwhelmed when he took off his helmet again. His pheromones flooded through her, and she could smell him much sharper than she had before. She gasped as he turned to her, and rings around his irises were starting to glow silver. She took a step back, colliding with the wall behind her as he bore down on her.

"Your eyes are ringed," he said in a rough growl.

Maya gasped as she reached up

to touch her face automatically. The rings only appeared when an Omega went into estrus, and she dropped her hand to her pump to check it. Without even scanning it, she could tell there was something wrong. Frantically, she unzipped her suit and reached inside, feeling broken metal. The pump had been damaged when the debris fell.

Panicked, she had only one thought, which was to get back to her ship and inject the suppressant before what remained in her system completely wore off. Already, she could feel herself going into estrus, which was completely normal. The longer an

Omega used a suppressant, the faster estrus came on when they stopped using it. She'd been on it continuously for almost five years, along with most of her life from age ten, aside from those few fateful days following her mother's death.

He was growling now, sniffing her and leaning closer. Part of Maya wanted to submit to him, to lean in and enjoy his embrace. The impulse scared her, and all it took was the memory of Thane holding her against the wall as he stole her innocence with the crowd surrounding them, uncaring and not doing anything to stop it, to remember exactly why Alphas were so dangerous. With a little bleat of terror, she darted under his arm and started running.

She was no match for him, especially if he was entering a rut, and she feared her estrus was starting him down that path. She made it as far she could but was only a few feeble steps out of the quarters before he caught up with her, reaching out to jerk her back against him and drag her back into the room.

He was frantic in his need as he peeled the E-suit from her before disrobing of his own after tossing her on the bed. Maya was afraid, but her own nature was starting to take over as well. She whimpered in fear as he dropped atop her, but when he buried his mouth against the scent gland in her neck and started licking, her whimper of fear turned to pleasure. She'd never felt anything like it. Heat suffused her body, along with an unfamiliar sense of well-being and an incredible amount of desire she could barely process.

"Omega," he said with a growl. He was harder and bigger than he had been, confirming he was entering rut.

Since Maya was rapidly reaching the pinnacle of estrus, her fear was fading now. As he started to undress her, she brought up her hands to help strip off the jumpsuit she wore underneath. She was soon naked before him, and while she was vulnerable, she also shivered with anticipation. She was afraid, but she was also certain he would protect her. That was her Alpha's job. She belonged to him, and in return, he cared for her and met her needs.

Part of Maya realized her thoughts were all inspired by the biological imperative of an Omega, and she would think differently of it once she was freed from the mind-altering effects of estrus, but the rational part of her was rapidly fading. Instead, she was responding to the proximity of an Alpha. *Her* Alpha. She grasped his shoulders, pulling her toward him. He was eager to comply, and his mouth touched hers a moment later.

Theirs was no simple kiss. It was like the ignition of an atom bomb, and intense warmth filled her. It was the fever that accompanied estrus, and if she didn't come soon, it could leave her physically damaged, so she sank into his arms, enjoying his touch and looking forward to the moment when he was inside her.

He kissed her with confident mastery, tongue blazing a trail to her mouth where no Alpha had been before. No one had ever kissed her like this. Before realizing so abruptly that she was an Omega, she'd had one Beta boyfriend as a teenager, but they'd mostly fumbled around with each other, and it had been a tepid experience at best. This kiss was the standard against which she would all measure all future kisses, and she was certain she would find any other wanting unless it came from the Alpha holding her.

He pulled away for a moment, but just to finish removing his clothes. During the brief time he was away from her, Maya's brain tried to reassert itself, reminding her why this was a bad idea, but she was lost in the throes of estrus and helpless to resist her desire. When he returned to her, he spent a moment licking her nipples and sucking them, making her toss her head.

She was flooded with slick, her thighs positively drenched with it. She'd never experienced anything like it before, and for a moment, she reveled in the experience. She'd spent all her life denying this side of her, physically suppressing it, and it struck her as entirely wrong to have done so. Lost as she was in the haze of being with her Alpha during estrus, she couldn't imagine ever returning to the suppressants.

"Sorry to be so fast, but I have

to be inside you." As he spoke, Remy reached between her thighs, two of his fingers pushing inside her insistently. He was clearly stretching her in preparation for his huge cock, and she appreciated it even as she grinded against him, wanting more. "Please, Alpha, I need you. Take me."

"Omega." The word sounded like a purr coming from him as he parted her thighs wider, giving himself maximum space before the head of his cock nudged against her opening.

Maya reached up, frantically grasping the dilapidated headboard of the bed that was starting to squeak. It was probably structurally unsound, but she couldn't bring herself to worry too much about it crashing under them. She was certain they would continue to fuck amid the debris if that happened.

He entered her suddenly, joining their bodies with a decisiveness that made her cry out from a combination of pleasure and a little discomfort. He was big, and it took her body a moment to adjust. Even though she was an Omega and made for this, it was still an intrusion that she had to adapt to before she could relax.

As soon as the discomfort faded, pleasure started to take over. He was filling her in a satisfying way she couldn't describe. Maya clutched his shoulders and strained against him as he grasped her hips, burying himself fully inside her to the hilt before pulling back to do it all again.

Over and over, he filled her, his cockhead striking against that special gland under her clit that contributed to her desire and spurred her need for pleasure. It released her scent as well, and it was almost as sensitive as her clit. The way he was thrusting into her provided maximum stimulation, and she screamed as she started coming around him.

He continued to pump into her,

clearly not yet close to his zenith. From what she understood of a proper mating, that wasn't uncommon. Her sole experience had been with Thane, and her brother had shot him before he could finish coming inside her and knot to breed her. For a moment, the terrifying scene returned to her mind, making her freeze and shudder.

The Alpha above her instantly responded, his expression growing concerned. "Am I hurting you?"

She shook her head frantically, not willing to explain now. She didn't want to remember that time in the past and have it risk tainting this moment with Remy.

She'd never expected to mate with an Alpha voluntarily, but now that she was in the moment, she wanted to fully appreciate and embrace it, to have memories to savor in the future.

At her reassurance, he increased his thrusts even more, practically pounding her into the bed. She was straining back against him with equal vigor, her fingernails digging into his shoulders until she felt the wetness of his blood around them. She tried to ease her touch, but she couldn't seem to make herself do so.

She was lost in the animalistic throes of passion, coming once more around his shaft. This time, when her sheath contracted around his cock, it started him twitching as well, and he swelled inside her. He filled her almost uncomfortably, but then he started to release his seed, and he briefly diminished in size as he spurted cum into her in several waves. As his cock finished contracting, the knot at the base formed, keeping him sealed to her, and she orgasmed once more.

She'd never known such ecstasy, and it left her fuzzyheaded. She was almost too unaware to realize he was frantically licking the scent gland at her neck, and it was only as his teeth scraped it that she realized his intent. "No." She shouted the word forcefully, making him jerk in response.

He pulled back, lifting up so he could look down at her, though their bodies remained joined. "No?" He still appeared somewhat bestial, though his rut seemed to be fading.

She shook her head. "Please don't bite me and claim me. I don't want to be any Alpha's Omega. I'll be trapped. Do you understand?"

He made a mewling sound as he looked at her throat with obvious desire before his brown eyes closed. He seemed to be gradually regaining control, and when he turned his head away, she breathed a shaky sigh of relief. They were still joined by necessity because of his knot, but at least he hadn't bitten her. She was still free.

The thought was unexpectedly disconcerting rather than pleasing. For a moment, she entertained the idea of how life would be if she surrendered to him, allowing Remy to make a claim on her and take her as his Omega. She was certain her life would be filled with passionate moments like this, but it would also entail being submissive to him and considered little more than his property. She couldn't abide the thought.

As soon as his cock softened

enough to allow him to start to pull away, she was pushing against him, wanting her freedom. Part of her wanted to remain, to stay locked with him until they were both ready to mate again, but she was afraid to give in to that temptation.

He allowed her to pull away, but he didn't allow her to leave. Instead, with a very Alpha-like growl of possessiveness, he pulled her into his arms and held her against him. She tried to remain stiff, but his nose buried against her neck, continuously sniffing her, was having a drugging effect in its own right, and she was afraid if she didn't escape soon, she would lose herself in estrus again.

Fortunately, such frantic mating took a lot out of both of them, and the Alpha was soon asleep behind her, snoring softly. Maya resisted the pull of exhaustion and the desire to stay with him, gradually escaping his hold over the next few minutes as she made small moves to avoid waking him.

When she was free, she quickly dressed and donned her E-suit again. She ran from the room down the corridor, finding Swish waiting for her near the conduit tubes. The CAP showed only concern in her expression and made no snarky comments. She rubbed against Maya's leg in a reassuring fashion for a moment before Maya got into the conduit.

She didn't bother taking time to climb the rungs. She simply put her hands and feet on the outside and slid down them quickly, pausing only long enough to navigate through the debris that had blocked them before when she reached that conduit. Moments later, she was back on her skid and then back in the sanctuary of *Eve's Sacrifice.*

She was trembling as she rushed to her quarters, digging through the nightstand until she found a syringe kit and one of the bottles of suppressant. Normally, she used it to infuse the pump with more when it needed replacing, but this time, she took a dose, drew it up quickly, and stabbed herself in the thigh to administer it. Part of the quick, painful dispensing of medication was desperation to suppress the estrus that she could feel rising again and part was punishment for having surrendered all her principles in the throes of animalistic passion.

Abruptly, she realized his seed was still inside her, and if she were in estrus, she would be fertile. Maya shuddered at the thought, knowing if she bore his child, he would never let her escape. He would claim her as his Omega, and that would be the end of her life. She would be his slave rather than her own person, and that was intolerable.

She moved to the computer, calling up options for emergency birth control. Fortunately, the computer had the components on hand to synthesize a remedy for her, and she swallowed it a few minutes later. It would kill all his sperm well before it reached her egg, thus preventing this lapse in control from ruining her life.

It was only after she had consumed the medication and curled up on the bed for a few minutes to recover from the experience that she allowed herself a moment of sadness for doing so. She couldn't help picturing what a child with her Alpha would look like, how it would be to hold and nurse him, to see him grow into a fine Alpha in his own right. Of course, he could be a Beta, but she had a difficult time imagining an Alpha like Remy fathering a Beta child.

It was just as likely to be an Omega girl, and she immediately rejected that thought. She refused to consign a child to live the kind of life she lived, and what she had done was for the best.

She had no doubt if her mother had the same option twenty-five years ago when she found herself mated by three Alphas when too vulnerable to refuse and left carrying the offspring of one, she would've done the very same. Maya could find no resentment at the idea if her mother had prevented the pregnancy from ever happening, though it would've meant Chase and herself would've never been born.

How she wished she could talk to her mother now, but Eve had been gone five years. The day of her mother's memorial had also been the day Maya learned the hard way she was an Omega, though her mother had done her the kindness of suppressing that for her since before puberty.

If only she'd warned her ahead of time, but Eve's passing had been unexpected when she was crushed under a load that had fallen off a skid at the warehouse where she worked. There had been no time to warn Maya, and the letter her mother had written for in such an event hadn't reached her until a couple of days later, when she was still recovering from Thane's attack in the hospital.

With a sigh, she sat up, knowing she'd done the right thing and pushing back any hint of regret. While Remy gave every appearance of being a fine man and a good Alpha, she still didn't want to be tied to him.

She left her quarters and went to the flight deck, quickly strapping herself into the pilot's seat. She hadn't gotten the terilalium jewelry from the *Helena*, and she was leaving with her cargo hold less than half-full, but it couldn't be helped. At least she'd earned enough to pay for her fuel passage back to the planets closer to the hub of the Coalition, and she would work on rebuilding her savings to try the Antares Belt again in the future.

She programmed her coordinates into the computer and was about to take off when she heard a thump. She looked up through the cockpit window and saw Remy on his skid blocking her path. If she moved forward, she would knock him off and likely leave him adrift if his thrusters' orientation system couldn't adapt and reorient him. She could back up and go around him, but something in his gaze was compelling, keeping her hand hovering on the shifter without engaging.

"Don't leave. Let's talk, please." His voice came through her cockpit via channel eight-seven-two. He sounded desperate, almost imploring, and she found her hand gradually dropping away from the shifter.

Feeling like a fool, she slowly engaged "Hover" again and lowered the bay door so he could enter. She braced herself to face him, unsure why she was giving him a chance, and why she wasn't doing the smart thing by running away when she had the opportunity.

CHAPTER FOUR

Remy rushed through her ship, reaching the cockpit only to find the door locked. "Open up. I want to see you in person." He sounded rough and demanding, and he instantly softened his tone, realizing that would only frighten her more. "Please, Maya. I'd like to speak face-to-face. Will you open the door?"

He truly expected her to remain unmoved, so it was a surprise when the door slid open a moment later. She was still seated in the pilot's seat, her arms crossed over her chest. Noticeably, she wore a holster with a laser pistol snugged inside, and he had the feeling she would use it if she felt afraid of him.

It was a relief to see her, almost immediately followed by displeasure. Breathing in her scent revealed she was on the suppressant again. He could barely pick up any indication she was an Omega now, except the rings around her eyes remained. He assumed it would take a while longer for them to fade, and it wouldn't happen until the optimal dose of suppressant had built up in her system once more. He shook his head in confusion.

"Why are you hiding what you are?"

She snorted at him. "That's an easy question for you to ask. As an Alpha, the world is yours to command. As an Omega, I'm considered your subordinate, and you can do what you want with me as long as you don't kill me. All Alphas are like that, and all Omegas are their victims. I refuse to live my life as a victim again, and I'm much happier not being an Omega."

He was stunned by her words, shaking his head. "It's not like that at all." As he spoke, he moved over to the copilot's seat, and Swish hopped out so he could sit down. He nodded his thanks to the CAP before turning back to Maya. "Omegas are for cherishing and protecting. Our job is to see to your every need and to keep you safe, to ensure you're loved, and to protect our offspring. That's my biological imperative."

She rolled her eyes. "Supposedly, but far too many Alphas find it easy enough to ignore that imperative and just take what they want. They regard Omegas as toys. When I'm in the throes of estrus, I have little common sense and rarely the ability to refuse anything. More than one Alpha will take advantage of that."

Sensing she spoke from experience, he had to resist the urge to surge to his feet and demand to know who had hurt her. He wanted to rip them apart, but he was certain any sign of violent anger on his part would just make things worse between them. He clutched the armrests of the seat he occupied, feeling the fabric start give under the pressure he exerted, so he loosened his hold slightly. "That happened to you?"

She hesitated for a moment before nodding. "My mother had given me a suppressant from before puberty, since she realized what I was. I never knew, so when she died unexpectedly, I didn't get my dose for a few days. It wore off right after my mother's memorial service."

Her eyes closed, and a tear streaked on her cheek. He wanted to reach out and brush it away, but he was afraid he would startle her, and she might shut down again. He needed to hear what had happened to her so he could find a way to overcome her fear and objections to allowing him to be her Alpha.

"I was in the middle of a crowded street when the estrus came over me. I was so confused and scared, and lost in grief at losing my mom, that I had no idea what was happening. I had no chance to feel any pleasure or respond to any biological imperative. It was terrifying.

"My brother Chase was there, and he was trying to help me. People thought I was ill until the Alphas appeared."

He scowled, trying to keep his tone level. "They smelled you?"

She shuddered. "I guess. It was clear all four of them intended to take me. Chase tried to fight them off, but the one in charge, Thane, took me from him. He slammed me against the building, and he forced himself on me with everyone around watching, and no one do anything to stop it. His friends planned to be next. They were lining up and getting ready."

He couldn't hold back the growl in his throat that emerged as a fierce roar. "I'll kill him."

She surprisingly didn't flinch from his angry tone. Her gaze was haunted though. "You're too late. Chase did that. When no one did anything, he snatched a gun from one of the enforcers standing around watching the entertainment and shot Thane. He shot the other three as well. Thane and two of them died, and the other one was permanently injured." She sounded uncaring about his fate.

He breathed a shaky sigh of relief, though he was feeling

slightly petulant that he wouldn't get the chance to exact his own revenge. "Bless your brother."

She looked down, shaking her head. She appeared to be on the verge of sobbing, but she drew in a ragged breath instead. "He should have just let them do what they wanted. The laws protect Alphas, not Omegas. They were moved by the biological imperative, supposedly trapped in rut and responding to my estrus. They were completely shielded by the law, and Chase wasn't.

"He was convicted of manslaughter for interfering and killing three of them. It didn't take long for an Alpha in prison to exact revenge, leaving me completely alone in this world." She looked up at him, her expression haunted. "Chase kept Thane from knotting inside me and fully breeding me, but at the expense of his own life ultimately. It wasn't worth it. I could have just taken a pregnancy preventative. They were easily accessible where we were."

He scowled. "I'm certain your brother was thinking more about the pain you were enduring, rather than preventing such a thing. He did the right thing."

She seemed surprised. "You truly believe that as an Alpha? You think it was okay for a Beta to come between an Alpha and the Omega he's intent on claiming? You'd be okay with those circumstances?"

He shifted in his seat, feeling uncomfortable. "Part of me is angered at the idea of anyone trying to interfere with me and my Omega, but you were being taken without pleasure and without consent. I know your brother did the right thing, regardless if he was a Beta. It was wrong for the spectators and enforcers not to try to stop the assault, leaving him no other choice."

She closed her eyes for a moment, appearing relieved.

When she opened them again, she eyed him doubtfully. "You aren't what I expected. I mean, for an Alpha, you seem like a decent man."

Damned by faint praise, he thought with a twist of his lips. "I try to be a decent man, and I'd like to think I would be a good Alpha to my Omega. My goal is to love her and cherish her, to keep her safe and satisfied, and always happy. I've been looking for my Omega all my life and for the last two years, completely forgoing any other sexual relationships. They're a waste of time when I know I can only be satisfied with an Omega. *My*

Omega." He hesitated for a moment before adding, "You."

She frantically shook her head. "I don't want to be any Alpha's Omega. I hate the status. I'm my own person, not a subordinate to you."

He frowned. "I would never consider you a subordinate to me. Don't you understand it's coded into my DNA to protect and love you?"

She shrugged a shoulder. "That might be your imperative, but the law is clear. I have no rights as an Omega, at least when it comes to Alphas' rights. They trump all my rights, and allowing myself to willingly mate with you, to be bound to you for life, would be agreeing to those terms. I refuse to be any man's slave."

He scowled. "I have no plans to enslave you."

Maya shrugged. "Your plans don't matter to me. I'm sorry to be so blunt, but it's the truth of the matter. I have my own plans, goals, and aspirations, and they don't include accepting anyone as an Alpha. I'm sure you can tell by now that I've returned to taking the suppressant, and I'll continue to do so."

He could feel her slipping away from him, and if he didn't handle it just right, he would lose all chance of being with her forever.

If she decided to leave the Antares Belt to return to more civilized space, he'd probably lose track of her. Now that she was within his grasp, and he recognized her as the Omega he'd been waiting for, he couldn't bear the thought. "I accept your decision then. There's no reason to rush off. We work well together, and I suggest we continue our partnership."

She eyed him warily. "I don't know if I can trust you."

That set his teeth on edge, but he reminded himself she had good reason to be distrustful of Alphas. Gritting his teeth, he took a deep breath to regain control of his anger. "I haven't harmed you, and

I won't. I'm sorry for rushing you through mating, but we were both willing participants."

She nodded, looking disconcerted. "I can't deny that. I've never been through a full estrus before, and I didn't realize how compelling it would be. I hold no anger toward you for submitting to your rut and acting on it. I was sending out clear signals, but I want to make it clear I won't be in that position again. I will continue to use my suppressant, and if you try to interfere, I'll leave. If I have to, I'll shoot you to do it."

His eyes widened at the threat, and he sensed she was sincere.

He'd known some strong Omegas before, but his was the strongest yet. Rather than be afraid, he felt a swell of pride, but he managed not to grin. He didn't want her to think he was mocking her when he took her seriously. "I understand. I'm simply suggesting we work together. As long as you're on the suppressant, I'll be able to control my urges."

He could still smell the Omega pheromones from her, and he could see the rings remained around her irises, but they were gradually fading. Likely, the silver would be gone by morning, and so would the enticing smell of her. He mourned the idea of it disappearing again, but he was also thankful there was an option that would allow him to maintain control and perhaps win her over. It was his only chance to be with her, and he was willing to do whatever it took to make that happen.

CHAPTER FIVE

Maya initially expected to regret her decision, and she was on her guard constantly for the first few days working alongside Remy. When he managed to control himself, once again treating her as he had before their joining, she gradually started to relax around him.

Her pump had been permanently damaged, so she was having to inject herself daily with the suppressant, and she was careful not to miss it, but as the days passed with his congenial company, him showing her the best side of him, more than once she hesitated before pressing the plunger to administer the medication.

Was she making the right choice to continue to hide what she was? She was unlikely to find a better Alpha than Remy, so would she regret it if she stuck with her plans and parted from him when they were finished filling the holds of their ships? She questioned that more frequently as she gave herself the suppressant, but she still managed to press the plunger each day.

They were working inside an old medical freighter today,

sorting through what was still viable and what had expired long ago. They were splitting the haul evenly, tossing things into their bags a little haphazardly, when Remy stilled. She looked over, realizing he was in a section of diagnostic tests. "What is it? Are they all bad?"

He shrugged. "Undoubtedly. They expired seven years ago, but it's the nature of the test." Hesitantly, he reached onto the shelf and handed her a box.

She took it, realizing quickly it was a saliva test to confirm pregnancy and gender, along with the complete genetic profile of the child one carried. She quickly passed it back to him. "I don't think we'll need those."

He sighed, looking regretful. "I don't suppose we will. You are preventing that somehow, aren't you?"

She nodded quickly. "I took a preparation shortly after we mated. It's a spermicide, so there was no chance of your sperm ever meeting my egg."

"Good." He didn't sound all that convincing as he said the words though. He looked sad and lost for a moment.

Maya had to blink back tears, and she quickly turned away from him to continue inventorying the medicine on the shelf in front of her. "I found a few things that are salvageable, but it's mostly bandages and wraps. All the medications have gone bad. It's a shame. This must've been destined for one of the colonies."

"Yeah, I hate to see all the medication that's gone to waste. And the fate of these poor passengers…"

She shuddered, recalling what they had found when they entered the ship. All the passengers on board had congregated near the cargo bay door, all wearing E-suits. They likely had planned to wait for rescue, and they must have put on the E-suits in case they were sucked out into space while they waited. Unfortunately, the ship had decompressed too rapidly, and it had killed them all. Not that they would've had much chance of rescue out here, especially with their broken ansible, which Remy confirmed wasn't working when he checked it to see if it was worth trying to salvage.

It was a common occurrence on these wrecks, and she was mostly inured against dead bodies, but she supposed today had been harder because there had been a mother and a little girl among the dead. They had clung to each other even in death, and it had been an upsetting sight.

"Do you want children someday?" asked Remy.

She blinked and then shook her head. "No. I wouldn't risk bringing a female child into the world as an Omega. I wouldn't put that curse on anyone."

He was frowning as he turned to look at her. "I guess it's a good thing your mother didn't feel the same."

She glared at him. "My mother was seduced by an Alpha who made promises and then ended up sharing her with his friends while she was in estrus and couldn't refuse. If she'd had the option to terminate, she probably would have, but they were on a backwater planet with limited medical supplies, just starting up their colony. I highly doubt she would've chosen to have us if she had another option."

He frowned. "Perhaps not, but I imagine she was happy to have you. She must've loved you very deeply."

Maya nodded. "I have no doubt about that, to be sure. She raised Chase and me with a lot of love. She even left the colony she was helping to build so we would have better opportunities, though we ended up in New Bacar. There were a few better prospects, but mostly for technological innovations. I suspect now that she moved us there when I was nine so she could have easy access to suppressants for both of us. She didn't want me to suffer the way she had." She closed her eyes, trembling for a moment. "I just wish she'd had a chance to tell me before she passed away, so I could have been prepared and avoided everything that followed."

He reached out, putting a hand on her shoulder. "I'm sorry you had to endure that."

Maya sniffed, refusing to cry. She'd cried for several days after the incident, but when she left the hospital, finally healed from the damage Thane had done to her as he held her and forced her, she had decided to set aside tears too. There had been one more round of crying when she received news months later that her brother was killed in prison, but she hadn't cried since. Tears would change nothing.

"Do you think your mother would approve of the path you've chosen then?"

Maya looked at him in surprise. "I'm sure she would have. She took the suppressant herself and gave it to me."

"Do you think she ever would have been open to finding another Alpha? I understand she had a very traumatic experience, but do you think it clouded her perceptions for the rest of her life?"

Maya's eyes narrowed, and she realized he was asking about her in a roundabout way. Maintaining the pretense, she said, "Clearly, my mother saw no reason to change her stance, or she would've stopped taking the suppressant."

"I'm not an Omega, obviously, but I don't think it's always like it was for you. If you aren't taking the suppressant, you aren't thrown immediately into such ferocious estrus when coming off it. You're more like yourself, and you have all your senses, but it doesn't change who you are fundamentally. It just completes your somehow."

She snorted. "Tell me that again when Alphas are the ones deprived of their rights to liberty because of biological imperatives." She turned away from him, continuing to work, and his silence lasted for the rest of the time they were on the ship.

It was only later, when she was back on *Eve's Sacrifice* and had time to think, that she wondered if he might be right. Was she doing herself a disservice by not allowing herself to fully be an Omega, to experience all aspects of it rather than just the intense estruses? She couldn't deny there was an element missing, and of course her senses were muted.

She reached for the syringe, realizing it was time to dose herself. She started to pull out the vial of suppressant but frowned. She looked down at it for a moment, considering her options. If she was going to allow herself to experience being an Omega, this seemed like a reasonably safe time. It would be better if she were alone, but if she really wanted to ensure she couldn't be happy with an Alpha claiming her, didn't she owe it to herself to experience the full gamut of the sensations?

She could always inject the suppressant if she changed her mind, so she set it aside and realized she was late to join Remy for dinner. They'd started eating some of their meals together, and she couldn't deny she enjoyed his companionship.

She suspected she could fall in love with him all too easily, and she worried that not administering the suppressant might hasten the process, but she was equally worried that maybe she was choosing to live her life as a reaction to events in her past. She had forcibly tried to shed the role of victim, but had she been self-imposing it all along without even realizing by cutting off part of herself deliberately?

She was still mulling it over

when she took the skid to his ship, parking it in his cargo hold before removing her E-suit to join him. He was waiting for her outside the cargo bay, and his nostrils flared as soon as she entered his space. She took a step back out of caution, but other than the quick inhalation of her scent, he seemed relatively unaffected and didn't mention that she suddenly smelled more Omega—which she was certain she did to him.

The suppressant had barely started to fade, but it would continue to do as the hours passed, though she didn't know if she would be pushed into such a frantic estrus as she had before, since she hadn't been taking it nearly as long this time.

"I hope you like fish. I synthicated trout."

"That sounds yummy." She followed behind him with Swish bringing up the rear, before taking the third seat at the table.

Swish sniffed the waiting plates curiously. "Times like these, I wish I had the ability to eat."

"It's unfortunate you don't," said Remy with clear sympathy.

After a moment, Swish flicked her ears. "I suppose it's for the best. At least I do not require biological nourishment to maintain homeostasis. As spotty as she is about my maintenance, I fear if I had to rely on Maya to remember to feed me, I would've starved to death long ago."

Maya play-hissed at the CAP as Remy laughed. Swish hissed in return, and then they both smiled at each other.

Dinner was delicious, but Maya was having a difficult time focusing on it. She felt itchy and hot, and she was certain it was a reaction to her pheromones surging naturally. More than once, she touched the scent glands at her wrists, each time aware of how his eyes widened and his nostrils flared. She realized she was deliberately enticing him with her scent, and her hand dropped away.

"You didn't take the suppressant." He was clearly having trouble speaking as he said the words with a hint of a growl.

She reached for her wrist again, this time unconsciously pressing her thumb against the gland. "I didn't. I thought I might experiment with seeing how it is without it. You raised a valid point this afternoon."

"Omega." He said the word with pleasure as he reached for her hand, bringing it to his mouth. His lips settled over the gland, and he started to suck it gently, which made Maya close her eyes and purr with pleasure.

"If you'll excuse me," said Swish in a prim voice as she jumped down from the chair, "I can see with this is going, and I have no need to witness that."

Maya laughed, though her mirth quickly faded as pleasure took over again. "I don't think I'm in estrus."

"No, you aren't. I'm not rutting neither. Is it all right if I make love to you?"

Maya bit her lip, undecided for a moment, though part of her had known this was inevitable when she came over without taking the suppressant. She nodded, and he stood up quickly, pulling her to her feet and leading her through his small ship to his bedroom. The door closed behind them with a hydraulic hiss, and it was just the two of them alone.

He stood behind her, her neck easily bared by the shortness of her haircut, so his lips could glide over the back of it. He moved to the side, his teeth lightly scraping against one of her scent glands, and she stiffened, uncertain if she wanted him to bite her or to keep going. Her rational brain insisted she reject the overture if he attempted to claim her, but the Omega side of her that was coming to life purred at the thought of him claiming her. She hated the confusion.

Fortunately, he found a way to distract her from that. Remy turned her in his arms, his hands going to the fasteners on her jumpsuit. He quickly unfastened it and slid it down, and then she helped him do the same. She had to strain on her tiptoes to reach the top fastener, so she could pull the section open, and then he was similarly disrobed.

They stared at each other for a moment, and she took time to appreciate his beauty. Before, when she'd been trapped in the throes of frenzied estrus, she hadn't been able to fully engage her senses to appreciate just how fine a specimen he was because she'd been too overloaded to process everything. Now, more in control of herself, she glided her hand down his stomach, tracing the ridges of his abs as she did so. "You're perfect."

He chuckled, though there was a bit of growl in the sound. "Not as perfect as you." He pulled her closer, lifting her into his arms so he could bend his head to kiss her. She wrapped her thighs around his waist, clinging to him as his mouth tenderly explored hers. This was much gentler and sweeter than their last joining, and though she couldn't say she preferred it, she appreciated the difference. She had a feeling that whether it was fast or slow, she was going to immensely enjoy sex with Remy under any circumstances.

He moved to the bed, lying down with her, and her legs dropped away from his waist. She was on her back, and he knelt over her, kissing her for several long moments before his mouth drifted lower, nibbling her neck prior to sweeping down to her breast. He took her right nipple in his mouth, sucking gently, while his other hand lifted to play with the left nipple, gently caressing in tandem the rhythm his tongue set.

She squirmed against him, lost in the sensations. This was so different from the last time she'd been with him, and it was far different from the horrible, scary experience she'd had with Thane. That event was fading into an unimportant memory, and she allowed it to do so. How she longed to forget about that incident, to let it reside in the past where it belonged. Each touch of his hand felt like it was healing her even as it was driving her closer to the peak of passion.

When his mouth moved lower still, she tensed in anticipation as his lips touched her mound. His tongue stroked her clit, and she squealed as she lifted off the bed. She produced some slick, but it wasn't anywhere close to the amount she had during estrus. This was regular sex, as normal as it became between an Omega and her Alpha, and there was no risk of pregnancy. She could just relax and enjoy it, so she focused on doing so.

Remy's mouth was talented as he brought her several orgasms over the next ten minutes, proving he had more stamina than average, and so did she. Perhaps this was normal for Omegas, and she'd have to remember to ask him later, when her brain was fully working again.

When he lifted his head, her pleasure was smeared on his face, and she pulled him closer to kiss him, curious what she tasted like filtered through his tongue. He groaned as she licked the appendage before sucking it and then pulled him closer still.

His cock brushed against her entrance, and she parted her thighs wider to invite him in. He was still thick, and it was a struggle to accept all of him when she wasn't in estrus, but he wasn't as big as he got in a rut. After a second, he slipped inside her, and it felt perfect. There was a straining sensation from being overfilled for an instant, but she quickly adapted and soon met each thrust of his hips eagerly.

She stared up at him, her gaze locked to his. She saw only tender concern and deep passion in his gaze. Even now, not in a rut, he was still driven to take care of her, to worry about her, and to please her. She was surprised to feel the same compulsions for him. Was this part of being an Omega, or was it simply a byproduct of being in love?

The thought should frighten her, but it didn't. Staring into his eyes, she realized she was falling for him. It no longer seemed so important that he was an Alpha, the thing she reviled most in the world. He was *her* Alpha, and that made all the difference.

This time when he swelled inside her, unleashing his release, he didn't knot. This was just sweet, sensual completion, and they gradually drifted down together in a hazy aftermath. She curled against him, stiffening when his lips stroked against the scent gland in her neck. Her thoughts were less clouded by passion now, and she wasn't ready for that step. "Don't bite me."

He stiffened before he relaxed against her, pressing just a tiny kiss to the scent gland before moving his head. "I wouldn't do that without your consent."

She nodded, believing him. She knew that in the throes of rutting, he might lose control, so there was a risk when they mated while she was in estrus, but like this, he could control his urges far easier.

Even without the frenzied edge from their previous mating, this had still been an amazing moment with him, and she accepted she had been cutting off part of herself with her decision to suppress the Omega inside. He had been right, but she didn't tell him that. He'd probably figured it out for himself, but there was no need to confirm she'd been wrong.

He'd realize that as soon as it became clear she was no longer using the suppressant—but she might reevaluate that decision as estrus approached, depending on how secure she felt with his ability to continue to restrain himself. If she was afraid he would lose control and bite her, claiming her as his without permission, she wouldn't hesitate to suppress her estrus again. She wasn't ready yet and might never be, but she also couldn't imagine losing Remy.

CHAPTER SIX

He was completely in love with her. Remy had known before that special night two weeks ago when she had surrendered to him so beautifully after stopping her suppressant. Over the last two weeks, he'd continued to fall deeper in love with her, and he hoped he was seeing signs of her growing love for him as well. At nights, they slept on her ship or his, always spending the nights together.

Most of their days were spent together as well, working side-by-side as they salvaged from the ships around them. There were so many shipwrecks that they would soon be ready to return to civilization with full hulls, and perhaps plans to come this way again. For now, they would be set for years, and he was pleased with their efforts, though as the hulls on each ship became more and more filled, his slight dread grew into anxiety.

When their job here ended, would their partnership dissolve, or would she stay with him? Could he accept her as his Omega without claiming her with his bite? It would be dangerous for her to reenter civilization without the suppressant if she refused to accept his mating claim. If she let him bite her, his scent would imprint on hers, and it would protect her from other Alphas.

If she were resistant to the idea, she would continue to use the suppressant, and he was certain that would change things between them. He would desire her no less, but a natural side effect of the suppressant was inhibiting her libido. She would probably still sleep with him out of pity, but she wouldn't lose herself with abandon like she did now. She would be doing it to please him with little pleasure in return. How could it become anything but a chore for her then?

It was a horrible situation in which to find himself, but he wanted to be supportive and allow her to make the choice. He wasn't so shallow that he was only with her because of sex. Even if she never wanted to make love again, he would still be beside her if she allowed it, but he dreaded how it would change the bond between them if it came to that.

It also set his protective urges on edge, imagining how vulnerable she would be if she were masking herself with a substance that might fail as it had unexpectedly with him. Any Alpha around could be driven to rutting and take her even if he was normally a decent guy. As much as she hated to hear the truth, the mating truly was a biological imperative, as the protective urge was meant to be, though not all Alphas cared enough about Omegas.

Some Alphas were selfish like that Thane, but all were wired to claim and possess an Omega, especially the right Omega who was a perfect match. He was certain he'd found her, but she had to be willing to accept his bite. If not, she would be at risk any time they were around people, and he'd never be able to relax. Not that he could be completely relaxed when he had an Omega to tend to, but he wouldn't have as much worry for her safety if she were securely marked as his mate.

Today, they were working beside each other to strip the outer shell of a hull when the CAP's eyes flashed red for a moment, and she looked at Maya. "There is a ship approaching. The *Talon*."

The name didn't mean anything to Remy and didn't seem to mean anything to Maya either.

"I suppose we should open communication," said Maya regretfully.

"There's plenty to share," said Remy, though he resented the intrusion of someone else. He and

Maya were just a couple of days away from finishing here, and he hated to have someone else infringing on his time with her. With luck, they would keep to themselves.

Her wrist comm beeped, and a face appeared a moment later. The visage sent dread spiraling through Remy as he recognized Aurelius Stahl's countenance projected from her wrist comm. He didn't move out of view in time, and Aurelius scowled. "Is that you, Cruz?"

Remy refused to cower behind his Omega and hadn't been planning to. He'd wanted to avoid a confrontation, but now that it was thrust upon him, he lifted her wrist comm to point the camera directly at him. "It is. I'm surprised to see you here in such a small freighter."

"You shouldn't be." The man had dark skin and white hair, and he wore a blistering scowl. "You were no doubt instrumental in enforcers discovering us smuggling just days after your departure from the ship. Or do you claim that's a coincidence?"

"It's a coincidence. I hope it's a coincidence that you're here at the same time as we are?" To his knowledge, Aurelius had no reason to track him, though the man seemed to believe he had betrayed him to the Coalition enforcers.

"We came to cash in on all the bounty around us. Who knew we would find a far greater prize? Revenge." Aurelius leaned closer to his camera, and his face loomed on the wrist comm. "I'm coming for you, Cruz, and I'm going to tear you apart with my bare hands."

Communication ended, and Remy quickly urged Maya onto to the skid. They'd taken to sharing one since they spent their nights together and departed from the same ship in the mornings, and her ship was the closest. "Hang on." He engaged full throttle on the skid, and though they were moving faster than was safe with the load they had, it was still painfully slow, especially compared to the small freighter Aurelius piloted.

The *Talon* was bearing down on them, and he tried to get more speed. He was about to dump the cargo itself, hoping it would give them the last boost they needed to get into *Eve's Sacrifice* and close the cargo doors, but the *Talon* collided with the skid a second later, sending them both flying.

He was unable to grasp anything to hold onto, and he was completely dislodged from the skid. Maya stumbled and fell, going over the side, but her hand clung to one of the runners of the skid as she reached out for him with her other. He was too far away though, and he continued to fly, propelled by the momentum of the crash. If he couldn't grasp something soon or orient himself to bring the thrusters in his E-suit online, he could spend the rest of his life drifting through space.

He scrambled to grab something, finally managing to grasp a big piece of detritus in time to see the bay door for the *Talon* open, and a pincer arm come out to grasp Maya before jerking her inside. He was chilled at the sight, and he half-expected the *Talon* to turn and engage its ionodrive to connect with the only boost gate in the system, but it slowed to hover.

He knew Aurelius and at least a few other crewmembers were Alphas, and the idea of his Omega being at their mercy, currently without her suppressant or his scent mark, spurred him to get to his feet. Once his orientation had leveled enough for the sensors to engage, he was able to turn on the thrusters in his E-suit to navigate toward the ship.

He approached slowly and cautiously, looking for place he could cling to on the hull while searching for a safe entry point that would allow him to slip inside without them noticing. If they'd observed him, surely they would have dealt with him by now, so they must not be watching. A chill ran through him as he wondered what they were doing that prevented them from surveilling the area around the ship.

CHAPTER SEVEN

Maya trembled as the pincer arms released her on the cargo floor. She fell to the metal on her hands and knees, gasping with fear. All she could think of was Remy floating through space, at its mercy, and that knowledge left her chilled long enough that she almost forgot she herself was at risk.

Only when a strong hand grabbed her shoulder and pulled her to her feet did she remember these people intended to harm her as much as they had Remy. If not, they wouldn't have risked injuring her by colliding with the skid.

She trembled as she looked up, finding two towering Alphas above her, flanked by a man who was clearly a Beta standing behind them. The Beta bore a strong resemblance to the dark-skinned man with the white hair, though his hair was black, and she assumed his natural color.

The one she identified as Aurelius from Remy's comments to him probably dyed his hair, because he wasn't old enough to have white hair yet. It was certainly a shocking contrast, and it made him look scarier. When he grinned, he revealed a gold tooth, and she couldn't help recalling ancient stories of pirates that her mother had read to her when she was a child. Her favorite had been "Peter Pan," but this guy made Captain Hook seem like a pussycat.

"Take off your suit."

Maya shook her head, clinging to it with desperation. If she removed her hood, they would smell she was an Omega. She hadn't taken her suppressant for two weeks, and though she should be at least a week from another estrus, they would still know what she was. They were Alphas, and if they were like the kind she knew, except Remy, they would take advantage of that.

She fought, but it did no good. The Beta male came forward after a nudge from the one who looked like him, and he stumbled a little before grabbing hold of her. Maya clawed at him and hit him in the solar plexus, making him bend forward. All that did was shove her toward the dark-skinned Alpha.

He grasped her in one arm and ripped off the helmet with the other. He and Aurelius both immediately stiffened as they inhaled deeply. A purr of satisfaction went through the one holding her, and she trembled.

"What is it?" asked the Beta,

looking worried.

"She's an Omega, Nico," said the one not holding her.

The Beta grimaced. "Surely, she bears Remy's mark then?"

The one not holding her practically salivated. "No. He's pathetic not to have claimed such a tasty morsel."

"Kirk, you should—" Whatever Nico planned to say, he was drowned out.

"This is an unexpected gift." Aurelius sniffed her, dragging her closer to lick the gland on her neck.

Maya almost vomited at the sensation and the wrongness of it. Even in the throes of estrus, she couldn't imagine ever finding it pleasurable to have that man touch her in such an intimate fashion.

"What about Remy?" asked Nico with an edge of desperation. "We should go after him."

"Forget him," growled Kirk. "He doesn't matter."

"Aurelius?" asked Nico. The man hesitated for a moment before shaking his head. "He's likely going to spend the rest of his short life drifting until he runs out of oxygen. Who cares? We have more important things to focus on."

"The salvage?" There appeared to be a hint of hope in the Beta's eyes.

Maya whimpered when Aurelius shook his head. "Her. She's worth more than a hull full of salvaged ship parts. We'll head back to civilization in the morning," said Aurelius.

"Until then?" asked Nico. He seemed stiff with dread.

Maya could relate, feeling it herself.

"I believe the Omega has some entertaining to do. We'll have some fun with her until we find an auction to sell her." Aurelius leered at her. "Are you close to estrus, Omega?"

She jerked way, fearing he'd let her more than she'd managed it on her own strength. She quickly realized he did so because it sent her flailing into Kirk's arms when she tripped over his foot.

"Tell me when you're going to be in estrus again, Omega," said Kirk in a commanding tone.

She trembled and tried to jerk away when Kirk's arms tightened around her, but he easily subdued her. She stomped backward with her boot to crush his toes, and he hadn't expected that. He howled with outrage and agony as he let go of her, and she started to run.

Unfortunately, Aurelius was able to catch up with her easily, since he was an Alpha. He grasped hold of her hair, arresting her flight and making her scalp sting enough to bring tears to her eyes. "Where are you going, little plaything? The fun is just beginning."

"Why do you get her first?" asked Kirk with a decidedly un-Alpha whine in his voice when he realized Aurelius was dragging her away.

"I'm the captain, and what I say goes."

As he dragged her past Nico, she made eye contact with the Beta male, and she could see his disgust at what was unfolding. "Help me. Please. Please!"

He stiffened, but then he looked away. He would be no assistance, but she hadn't really expected him to be. No one else had acted when Thane had raped her years ago, other than her own brother. If it had been another Omega who wasn't his sister, she doubted Chase would have had the courage to do anything either. Alphas could be bullies, and everyone tended to fear them.

She was grateful Remy wasn't that kind of Alpha. Contrasted with these two or Thane, she realized she was unfairly judging him and holding back from allowing him to claim her because of her experiences with men like this. Remy was nothing like these Alphas, and if she managed to escape this, she would happily accept his bite on her to fuse their scents and gain the protection of being his Omega.

He dragged her into small quarters that were unkempt and smelled foul. She wrinkled her nose, especially when he pushed her onto the bed. He clearly wasn't going to bother with anything like foreplay, because he had her on her hands and knees. He pushed her down hard and rough, his hands going to her jumpsuit. She screamed her outrage when he ripped it open near her crotch with his hands a moment later, not even bothering with the front closure.

The position forced her face against the pillow, and she was having trouble breathing. She turned her head, struggling to draw in a deep breath that didn't smell like the unwashed bedding and terrible body odor permeating the room. As she did so, her gaze fell on a knife on the nightstand.

It was just laying there for anyone to grab, including a desperate Omega. She simply had to be able to reach it. She stretched out her arm, but she wasn't quite close enough. She'd have to wriggle away and get ahead a few inches. She turned her head, looking up at Aurelius. He wasn't looking down at her. He was too focused on pulling his cock from his pants.

It was hard and big, and she shuddered at the thought of it entering her when she had no slick to ease its passage. That was one of many reasons the idea of him taking her disgusted her.

She refused to allow another man to impose his will upon her, and when he started to bend down, she kicked back with her foot, colliding with his jaw. That was enough to send him stumbling back for a moment, though he looked more stunned than in pain. It also gave her an opportunity to scramble forward, and she grasped the handle of the knife.

As he reached out for her ankle and pulled her toward him, flipping her onto her back, he was clearly angry. His rage was no match for her own, and she didn't allow herself to think about it as she brought up the knife and rammed it under his chin and upward as hard as she could while he bent down to face her. Surely, she must've struck his brain.

With a groan, he collapsed backward as convulsions made his body twitch. He flopped on the deck in a series of seizures, heels drumming the floor before his body became utterly still.

Maya let out a sob, but it was

one of brutal glee rather than sadness. She'd bested him, preventing him from taking what he wanted from her. She had not even a flicker of remorse that he was dead.

She got to her feet, reluctantly approaching to make sure he was in fact gone, but when she kicked him, there was no response. With a deep breath for courage, she bent down and grasped the knife handle, tugging it from his body. It was a gruesome, squishy business that made her want to puke, but she couldn't face Kirk without being armed in some fashion.

As she finally extricated the

knife, she heard a scraping sound outside the door. She braced herself to confront Kirk as it started to open. She brought the knife back, prepared to ram it into him just as ruthlessly as she had Aurelius. She wouldn't let another Alpha use and hurt her.

CHAPTER EIGHT

Remy had been looking for an entry point, so he was wary when the bay door suddenly opened. It was too easy, and he reached for the laser pistol in his holster as he entered cautiously.

He stood in the cargo bay for a moment, looking around until Nico Stahl stepped out of the shadows. He lifted his gun higher. "Where's Maya?"

"Don't shoot. I'm the one who

let you in." Nico held his hands out at his sides. "Aurelius has her in his quarters, and you have to stop that. He has no right to force anyone, Alpha or not."

Remy abruptly recalled Nico had been one of the few crewmembers he'd actually gotten along with when he had flown on the *Aurelius*. The Beta man was naturally humble and compassionate, and he wondered not for the first time how Nico had found himself tagging along behind Aurelius committing all sorts of sins and tragedies.

"How do I find her?" Remy tightened his hold on the pistol but wasn't pointing it at Nico now.

"Down the corridor, to the right. I'll show you, but I can't help you take him out. He's my brother, you know?"

Remy nodded grudgingly, understanding the perspective. "Who else is aboard?"

"Just Kirk O'Donnell. We were the only three who managed to escape the Coalition enforcers' raid. Did you turn us in?"

He snorted. "No, and why would I? I didn't want to get involved in criminal activities, but I didn't go running to the enforcers to tell on you either. I couldn't care less what you do as long as you don't hurt anyone.

Aurelius has crossed the line though, Nico. I know you won't help me stop him, but you won't be able to stop me from ending him if it comes to that. You understand?"

Nico swallowed, looking nauseated as he nodded. "What he's doing isn't right."

"Then take me to him."

They exited the cargo area, and Remy realized Nico was still on his guard, so Kirk could be anywhere. They soon encountered him as they turned a corridor, finding him standing near a set of closed doors. He inferred Kirk was waiting outside Aurelius's quarters to have his turn with Remy's

Omega.

Rage filled him, and he rushed forward, forgetting all about shooting the man as his body collided with him. Before he could unleash his rage, a weapon discharged, and a large hole appeared in Kirk's forehead as he went still.

Remy looked over at Nico, who was replacing his gun in his holster. "I thought you weren't going to get involved?"

He shrugged. "He's not my brother. I said I wouldn't help with Aurelius. I owe nothing to Kirk. He always was a terrible bully and got what he deserved." With those words, Nico turned and walked away, clearly done with all of it.

Remy waited to make sure he wasn't going to return or change his mind for a moment before approaching the door. He had to bypass the security features, so it took a few minutes. He got to work, using his wrist comm to help determine the schematics of the locking mechanism and where to disconnect. Eventually, he grew tired of that and got his laser pistol, shooting the entire mechanism. With a wobbling, screeching sound, the hydraulic doors opened, though the hiss was decidedly shrill.

As he started to step inside, he

saw a knife coming from the corner of his eye. Acting on instinct, he grabbed the wrist holding it and dragged the assailant closer. He'd expected Aurelius, but he recognized her scent even before he touched her. He pulled her against him and took the knife from her, tossing it aside.

She collapsed against his chest, and he held her as she sobbed, his gaze moving over to Aurelius's body. Pride filled him from her taking care of herself and preventing Aurelius from raping her. He held her against him for a long moment until she calmed down, and when she seemed composed enough, he let go of her to fetch her E-suit. It was still in one piece, though he saw the rip in her jumpsuit, and rage filled him again. "Did he hurt you?"

She shook her head. "He didn't really get a chance to. I stabbed him." There was pleasure in her expression, and it only added to his pride in her.

He leaned forward and pressed a kiss to her mouth. "I'm proud of you for taking care of yourself. I'm sorry I wasn't here to shield you from him."

She frowned up at him. "It's hardly your fault, Remy. You were thrown off the skid. We weren't expecting to be attacked."

He nodded, though he still bore Alpha's guilt for not protecting his Omega better. "I'm relieved to know you can take care of yourself. I'm proud of you, but we need to get out of here. I don't know if Nico will be so benevolent as to just let us leave when he realizes you've killed his brother."

She glowered. "He had it coming. I regret nothing."

He put his arm around her waist, squeezing gently. "I don't regret it either, but Nico might not let us walk away. If he interferes, I'll have to kill him, which I'm loath to do. He's a decent enough sort, considering his family and occupation."

They exited Aurelius's quarters, and he looked around but saw no sign of Nico. He took her hand, leading her to the cargo bay, and they still didn't run into Nico. "Is your suit functional?" He waited while she ran a diagnostic and nodded before he reached over to close the inner doors of the airlock.

When she was ready, he pressed the outer hull door, allowing them to exit into space. Using the thrusters on their E-suits, they navigated to his ship, which was closest. Once they were aboard, he locked it down tight and brought his weapons online, pointing them at Nico's ship in case the Beta decided to get revenge for his brother.

He watched with satisfaction as the ship started to accelerate, an ionospace gateway opening a second later before the *Talon* disappeared through it. He didn't anticipate seeing Nico again, and he certainly wouldn't run into Kirk or Aurelius, since they were dead.

He turned to Maya, pulling her against him as he sank into the pilot's seat, pulling her onto his lap. "Are you all right?"

She nodded, but then she stiffened in panic. "I don't know where Swish is. She was on the skid before that ship hit us.”

“We’ll find her.” He turned to the computer, recalibrating the sensors to find Swish. The system soon locked on, and he instructed the ship to follow the path.

They passed a few of the shipwrecks before exiting the main congestion. They followed Swish’s trail into empty space, rapidly catching up with her. He used the pincer arm to bring her board, and she soon joined them in the cockpit. She appeared unbothered by her adventure when she sat down and examined Maya critically before jumping onto her lap and rubbing against her chin as she purred. “Are you bleeding?"

"It's not my blood," said Maya as she hugged Swish. "I'm sorry we didn't find you sooner. We had to deal with them."

"I figured that might be the case. I knew you'd get me eventually."

"Not even a little doubt?" asked Remy.

The CAP looked at him, her eyes impassive. "I completely trust Maya, as long as we aren't talking about maintenance, and you seem all right, for a human male."

Remy laughed as he reached out to stroke the CAP on her ear. "You're all right too, Swish."

CHAPTER NINE

It didn't take them long to decide to leave the area, since their cargo holds were almost filled, and they had no idea if Nico would be contacting the authorities to send them back this way. Remy had deemed it unlikely, but Maya wanted to be cautious and depart, so he hadn't objected.

Now, they approached the planet they had identified as the best chance to sell their cargo, taking the path directed to them from Flight Control on the planet below. As they moved toward one of the larger cities, her tension rose. "I can't go out there unmarked without the suppressant."

He nodded. "I thought of that, but I wanted to let you decide how to proceed. If you want, you can wait on the *Raven*, or you can take the skid to *Eve's Sacrifice*. One ship can remain in orbit, and then I'll take down the other to sell the contents on the second one."

Her ship was being towed behind his, which had slowed their progress significantly with the ships being of similar size, but he'd been unable to let her out of his sight long enough for her to pilot her ship. He'd said he needed the reassurance of holding her and having her nearby.

Maya had understood when he expressed his needs, overlooking his bossy tone when he directed her to remain with him. She was capable of fighting and standing up for herself, but she was also capable of yielding when the situation warranted. She had enjoyed the reassurance of his arms as well after the sordid experience with Aurelius.

It was necessary for both cargo holds to be emptied and sold, and it made no sense to remain in orbit above the planet while he went down below. Licking her lips before drawing in a deep breath for courage, she said, "I think you should just bite me."

His eyes widened. "Are you certain?"

Maya nodded as she moved closer to him, once more sitting on his lap. "I realized in the middle of the situation that you aren't like the other Alphas. I knew it before, but I really *accepted* and *believed* it without fear. Finally. You're safe, and I love you. There's no reason I shouldn't accept your mark and be protected from other Alphas. I want to, because I love you."

He sagged, letting out a harsh sigh. "I was afraid I was the only one in love. You have no idea how much it pleases me to hear you say that. I love you too, and I'd be delighted to give you my mark."

Maya pushed down the shoulder of her torn flight suit, which was another article she'd need to replace when she was back on *Eve's Sacrifice*. It was harder to bite her unless he was sexually aroused, so she reached between their bodies to stroke his cock from the outside.

When he groaned, she brought her hand up to his flight suit and opened the fasteners, slipping her hand inside so she could grasp the hard length of him. He was more than her hand could accommodate and allow her fingers to still touch, so she stroked him as best she could.

She was getting aroused by touching him, and his hand went to the ripped section of her jumpsuit, fingers dipping into her pussy to coax her slick to present. They didn't have time for a full mating, so this would have to do for now.

She stroked him closer to completion as he fingered her. As their arousal grew, his licks and sucks on her scent gland grew more intense, until his teeth were gliding over the area, raking lightly. When his cock twitched, tightening before he released an orgasm that splashed over her hand, his teeth penetrated her skin.

There was a sharp pain, but it was quickly overwhelmed by pleasure as she came from his fingers playing with her clit and pushing her over the edge. The bite only added to her orgasmic bliss, and she cried out as she became his Omega.

Afterward, he held her against him in a soothing fashion, lightly kissing her and still stroking her thigh, though he'd stop touching her sensitive pussy for the moment. "Are you all right, Maya?"

She nodded. "I'm fine.

Wonderful, in fact." She felt a new sense of peace settle over her. She's never known anything like it. She hadn't realized what was missing until it was filled in, and now she was completely whole, marked by her Alpha as she was.

"You're my Omega now. I hope you never regret that decision, Maya." He sounded concerned.

"I can't imagine I ever will." She took a deep breath, forcing herself to slide away from him since they were being contacted by Flight Control again. It was their turn to navigate to a landing spot. "We have things to attend to, but later, I want to spend far more time strengthening your claim."

He chuckled. "It won't be as strong as it could be until your next estrous, but I'm certainly willing to practice until then. My scent is enough to protect you now though."

She trailed her fingers down his neck. "I love you." She kissed him before he turned away from her to pilot their ships to the designated landing spot. They had business to attend to, and pleasure would come later. She was looking forward to it now that she had an idea of how fulfilling it was to mate with *her* Alpha.

EPILOGUE

Two years later

"The little human requires sustenance," said Swish as she jumped onto Remy's lap. "Maya wanted me to tell you she'll join you shortly."

"Thanks, Swish." He stroked the CAP's ears as he stared out at the expanse of space in front of them. It was just the four of them on the ship—Swish, him, his Omega, and their two-month-old daughter. Briefly, he recalled how frightened Maya had been when she'd learned she was pregnant, but by the time their baby arrived, she'd seemed relatively calm about the idea of raising an Omega daughter.

He was still nervous as hell about the prospect, but he was determined they would protect little Neve and keep her safe. She wouldn't have to grow up being suppressed. When it was time, she could decide if she wanted to take the suppressant, but he was determined she would grow up knowing who and what she was, so she wasn't left in the same vulnerable position as Maya had been. Eve had likely done what she thought was best, but he didn't agree with keeping Neve in the dark, and neither did Maya.

He waited for a few minutes until Maya appeared with Neve latched on. She sat down in the copilot's seat of *Eve's Sacrifice.* "Did you find the coordinates?"

"I did. That research you paid for really was worth it." He made the concession grudgingly, since he'd protested at her spending such a large amount of credits on what he'd considered dubious information from someone they had met in a trading market a few months before. The intel had turned out to be sound, and they would soon reach another sector full of shipwrecks from travelers who hadn't paid enough attention to a local asteroid belt.

They hadn't been back to Antares and might not for a while, since it was so remote and away from civilization. He preferred to stay closer to easier areas to travel until Neve was older, so they had pursued the information she paid for, and he was big enough to admit he'd been wrong.

"It looks like it might be quite a haul, according to the sensors." He tapped one lightly. "This sure is an upgrade from the *Raven*." They had sold the *Raven* the night they sold all their other cargo, deciding they didn't need two ships. His ship had been superior in some ways, but Maya's had the better A.I. system, and he knew the ship alone was important due to its name and sentimental value, so he had given up the *Raven* without her having to ask.

Technically, they didn't need to undertake another salvage operation, since they were comfortable for the time being, but neither liked to be idle, and they certainly couldn't imagine settling down on one of the Coalition planets in a crowded colony. This was the life they loved, and they were determined to share it with Neve.

It also appealed to his paternal instincts, since it would be easier to keep her safe growing up in places like this, though he knew he couldn't shelter her completely from the world. That was a problem to deal with in the future though. Right now, he just wanted to bask in the happiness he'd found with his Omega and their daughter.

He took her hand as the ship exited ionospace, coming to a slow halt before hovering. The ships around them promised to yield enough resources to be more than worth the money she'd paid for information, and she gave him a smug grin.

He returned her grin, without the smugness. "It is quite amazing. You were right, love."

Maya nodded, clearly pleased. "This should keep us busy for quite a while."

"No doubt, but I suggest we start tomorrow morning." He feigned a yawn and stretched. "Is it about bedtime?" he asked with a lascivious leer that was only partially feigned. The idea of having her body underneath his revved him up just as it always did, though she wouldn't enter estrus again until she was done breastfeeding. They could still have amazing sex when they weren't caught in the throes of their biological imperatives.

She chuckled as she looked down at Neve, who was currently

dripping milk from the side of her mouth as she dozed. "I think she agrees, and you know it's always a good idea to sleep when the baby sleeps."

"Sleep. Yes. Eventually." With a throaty chuckle, he stood up and followed her from the cockpit. He paused to look back at Swish, who took his seat. "You have the ship, Swish?"

She nodded. "Everything is fine. I much prefer to stay here rather than overhear what you two humans do to each other." With an uninterested flick of her tail, she turned her back on him, her gaze focused on the darkness of space before them, filled with the floating debris from the shipwrecks waiting to be salvaged. The ship was in good hands.

And Maya was in good hands as well. It was his duty to love and care for her, to cherish and protect her, and he'd spent every day of their life together so far living up to that. He intended to continue to do so, and as her hands enfolded his a short time later to take him to the bed after placing Neve in her crib, he soon remembered he was in good hands as well. Soft, sweet, feminine hands that could bring incomparable pleasure or sensual torture, and they were hands to which he gladly surrendered.

ABOUT JUNO

Juno Wells grew up on Florida's Space Coast, watching the shuttles take off from Cape Canaveral. When she hit college, her childhood fantasies about space travel turned highly romantic. Now her mind reels with space adventures of fantastic alien lords in distant galaxies, and the Earth women they love.

Wells' stories explore the complex, sensual relationships between inhabitants of different star systems. There are always happy endings just as there is always a new world to explore.